# Karen's Goodbye

## Also in the Babysitters Little Sister series:

*Karen's Witch*

*Karen's Roller Skates*

*Karen's Worst Day*

*Karen's Kittycat Club*

*Karen's School Picture*

*Karen's Little Sister*

*Karen's Birthday*

*Karen's Haircut*

*Karen's Sleepover*

*Karen's Grandmothers*

*Karen's Prize*

*Karen's Ghost*

*Karen's Surprise*

*Karen's New Year*

*Karen's in Love*

*Karen's Goldfish*

*Karen's Brothers*

*Karen's Home Run*

## Look out for:

*Karen's Carnival*

*Karen's New Teacher*

*Karen's Little Witch*

# Karen's Goodbye

## Ann M. Martin

Illustrations by Susan Tang

Hippo

Scholastic Children's Books,
Scholastic Publications Ltd,
7-9 Pratt Street, London NW1 0AE, UK

Scholastic Inc.,
555 Broadway, New York, NY 10012-3999, USA

Scholastic Canada Ltd,
123 Newkirk Road, Richmond Hill,
Ontario, Canada L4C 3G5

Ashton Scholastic Pty Ltd,
P O Box 579, Gosford, New South Wales,
Australia

Ashton Scholastic Ltd,
Private Bag 92801, Penrose, Auckland,
New Zealand

First published in the US by Scholastic Inc., 1991
First published in the UK by Scholastic Publications Ltd, 1994

Text copyright © Ann M. Martin, 1991

Cover illustration copyright © Dennis Ryan, 1994

ISBN 0 590 55646 0

Typeset by A.J. Latham Ltd, Dunstable, Beds
Printed by Cox & Wyman Ltd, Reading, Berks

10 9 8 7 6 5 4 3 2 1

*The author gratefully acknowledges*
*Stephanie Calmenson*
*for her help*
*with this book.*

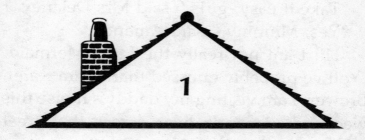

# Amanda

*S*PLASH! Guess where I am. I am in Amanda Delaney's really big swimming pool!

"I'm the Little Mermaid!" I said. "I am going to hunt for treasures!" I held my nose and —

"Wait. Who will I be?" asked Amanda.

"You can be my friend, Flounder," I said. "Your job is to watch out for the . . . the shark! The shark is after us!" I shouted.

"Eeek!" yelled Amanda. We were yelling

and giggling and racing around the pool.

"Take it easy, girls," said Mrs Delaney.

"Yes, Mummy," said Amanda.

Hi! I am not really the Little Mermaid. (You've probably guessed that.) I am Karen Brewer. I am visiting my daddy's house this weekend. Amanda lives across the street and one house down from Daddy.

When I visit Daddy, I play mostly with Hannie Papadakis. She is one of my two best friends. (Nancy Dawes is my other best friend. Together we are the Three Musketeers!) But today was Sunday and Hannie was visiting her grandma.

I do not play with Amanda much when Hannie is around. Hannie does not like Amanda *at all*. She thinks Amanda is a snob. And I suppose she is a little.

I might turn into a snob, too, if I lived in a house like Amanda's. First of all, right in the front hall is a *real* fountain. It is shaped like a fish standing on its tail. The fish spits water into a little pool. (I think the fountain is funny!) In the back garden are *two* tennis courts and the swimming pool. The pool is bright blue, with two sets of steps, a water slide, and a diving board!

That is not all. Amanda has a white Persian cat named Priscilla. She goes around telling everyone in the world how her cat cost four hundred dollars. That makes Hannie so, so angry.

But I get on fine with Amanda. Even if she does say snobby things sometimes. (I ignore her.) And even if she is a little older than me. (I'm seven. Amanda is eight.)

"I think we scared the shark away," said Amanda. "Now what should we do?"

"Let's have a penny hunt!" I said. Mrs Delaney always keeps a cup of pennies at the side of the pool for us.

We each took a handful and dropped them into the water.

"On your marks. Get set. Go!" I called.

We ducked underwater and scooped up as many pennies as we could hold. Then we

put them at the side of the pool and ducked down again. We kept going until no pennies were left.

"Let's see who got the most," said Amanda.

We each reached for the same pile of pennies.

"Those are my pennies," said Amanda.

"No they're not. They're *my* pennies!" I said.

Amanda and I looked at each other. Then we started giggling. We had put all our pennies in the same place.

"I won!" we shouted together.

"Hey, your lips are turning blue," I said. "You look like the Slimy Monster From the Sea!"

"Your lips are blue, too," said Amanda.

I was really feeling cold. That is because the sun was going down. Uh-oh. If the sun was going down, it meant it was getting late. And if it was getting late, it meant that Mummy would be coming to take me and my little brother, Andrew (he's almost five), back to her house.

"I've got to go," I said. I grabbed my things and ran to Daddy's.

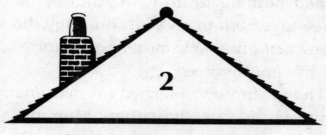

# One-Ones and
# Two-Twos

**H**onk! Honk! I got back to Daddy's and dried off just in time. Mummy was there to take Andrew and me back to her house.

"'Bye! See you in two weeks!" we said to everyone at Daddy's house.

I suppose you are wondering why Mummy and Daddy live in different houses. Well, I will tell you.

It started a long time ago when Andrew and I were one-ones. We lived in one house with one mummy and one daddy.

But then Mummy and Daddy decided

they did not want to be married any more. It had nothing to do with Andrew or me. They love both of us a lot. But they did not love each other any more. So Mummy and Daddy got divorced.

Then Mummy married a man named Seth. He is our stepfather. Mummy and Seth live in a little house not far from Daddy in Stoneybrook, Connecticut. That's where Andrew and I live most of the time. A little house is just fine because the only people in it are Mummy, Seth, Andrew, and me.

Oh, yes. There are three animals. There's Midgie, Seth's dog, and Rocky, Seth's cat, and Emily Junior, my pet rat.

Daddy got married again, too. He married a woman named Elizabeth. She is our stepmother. Daddy and Elizabeth live in a huge mansion. Andrew and I live there every other weekend and for two weeks in the summer. It's a good thing the house is so big. An awful lot of people live there.

These are the people at the big house: Daddy, Elizabeth, and Elizabeth's kids (our stepbrothers and stepsisters). They are Charlie and Sam, who are so old they go to high school; David Michael, who is seven; and Kristy, who is thirteen. Kristy is one of my most favourite, favourite people. Sometimes she babysits for Andrew and me. She is a very good babysitter. She even started a business with her friends called The Babysitters Club. Kristy is the chairman.

Wait. I have not finished. There are more people at the big house. Emily Michelle is my adopted sister. Daddy and Elizabeth adopted her from a faraway place called Vietnam. She's two and a half. And I like her even if she did take my place as the littlest girl in the house. (I named my rat after her.)

Then there is Nannie, Elizabeth's mother. (She is my stepgrandmother.) She came to help take care of Emily Michelle. But really she helps take care of everyone. I love Nannie!

There are animals at the big house, too. There's Shannon, David Michael's puppy.

There's Boo-Boo, Daddy's fat, mean, old cat. There's Goldfishie. That's Andrew's fish. And Crystal Light the Second. She is my fish.

So Andrew and I have two houses, two families, two sets of pets. And because we do not like to carry a lot of stuff back and forth, we have two of almost everything else. I have two bicycles. I have two stuffed cats. (Goosie lives at the little house, Moosie lives at the big house.) I have two sets of clothes, including two pairs of pink trainers and two unicorn shirts. I even ripped my special blanket, Tickly, in half so I could have two pieces — one for each house.

This is why I call us two-twos. (I thought of that name after my teacher, Miss Colman, read my class a book called *Jacob Two-Two Meets the Hooded Fang*.)

Would I want to be a one-one again? Sometimes, like when something I need is at one house and I am at the other. Or when I am at the big house and I miss the people at the little house.

But mostly I like being a two-two. I have the most totally wonderful family there ever was!

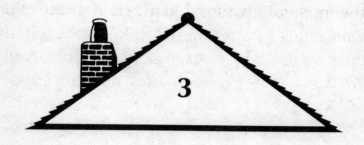

# Hannie's Announcement

It was a rainy Wednesday morning. Yuck! I pulled up my rain hood and hurried into Stoneybrook Academy.

"See you later, Mummy!" I called.

"Thanks for the lift, Mrs Engle," said Nancy.

Sometimes Nancy and I travel to school together. Nancy lives next door to Mummy's house.

Nancy and Hannie and I are all in the second grade. Our teacher, Miss Colman, is the best there is. You see, I am the youngest in my class because I skipped a grade. So sometimes I forget things. Like I get excited and forget that we are not supposed to yell in class. Miss Colman does not get cross. She just says, "Indoor voice, please, Karen."

Or I forget to wear my glasses. I have two pairs. Blue for reading and pink for the rest of the time (except when I am sleeping). If Miss Colman sees me squinting, she taps her own glasses to remind me to put mine on.

And sometimes I'm a show-off, like when I kept winning spelling tests. Miss Colman did not embarrass me in front of the whole class. She just took me aside and talked to me quietly about being a good winner.

Do you want to know something? I think that I would get excited and yell and forget to put my glasses on and act like a show-off even if I had not skipped a grade. That's just the way I am.

Nancy, Hannie, and I were early, so we had time to talk before class started.

"Guess what! I have a Surprising Announcement to make!" said Hannie. (That is what Miss Colman says when she has special news.)

"Hurray! What is it?" I said. I love Surprising Announcements.

"Amanda Delaney's family is moving!" said Hannie. Her smile was about a mile wide. Remember — she and Amanda are mortal enemies.

I was too upset to say anything. No one had told me the Delaneys were moving.

"Where are they going?" asked Nancy.

"They're going to a place called Lawrenceville," said Hannie.

"That's not very far from here," said Nancy.

"Too bad," said Hannie. "Amanda is going to be more of a snob than ever. Her new house is even bigger than the one she lives in now."

"Good morning, class," said Miss Colman. "Everyone please be seated."

14

I was glad it was time to go to our seats. And I was extra glad that I did not have to sit next to Hannie. Hannie and Nancy and I used to sit together in the back row. That was before I got my glasses. Then Miss Colman put me in front with Natalie Springer and Ricky Torres. (Ricky is my husband. We got married once at break.) Ricky and Natalie wear glasses, too.

It really was a good thing that I did not have to sit next to Hannie now. When we sat together we used to pass notes to each other. If I wrote a note now, it would be a mean note. It would say,

DEAR HANNIE,
    BOO. BOO. BOO TO YOU! AMANDA IS MY FRIEND. YOU DO NOT HAVE TO BE SO HAPPY SHE'S LEAVING.

                                    KAREN

But I would not want to send that note.

I would not want Hannie to know she made me feel bad.

But I did not turn around once all morning. And at break I did not play with Hannie Papadakis!

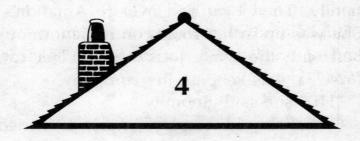

# A Party for Amanda

"Rise and shine, Moosie!" I said. It was Saturday morning at the big house. I usually love waking up at the big house. But today something was making me sad.

"I remember," I said to Moosie. "Amanda is moving away."

I had talked to Amanda on the phone the night before. I promised to visit her first thing in the morning.

I put my clothes on really fast and went down to the kitchen. I ate about three mouthfuls of Rice Krispies.

"See you later!" I called to my big-house family. Then I hurried over to Amanda's. She was up in her room, on her enormous bed with the white lace canopy. Her cat, Priscilla, was keeping her company.

"Hi," she said gloomily.

"What should we play?" I asked. (I tried to sound super cheerful.)

"Maybe we should practise saying goodbye to each other," said Amanda with a sigh.

"No way! I hate goodbyes," I said.

Here's how many goodbyes I've said in my life. (And I'm only seven.)

— I say goodbye to Mummy and Seth and Emily Junior every other Friday when I go to Daddy's.

— I say goodbye to Daddy and Kristy and all the people at the big house every other Sunday when I go back to Mummy's.

— I had to say goodbye to David Michael's dog, Louie. That is because he got so old, he had to be put to sleep.

— I had to say goodbye to my first goldfish, Crystal Light. She died.

— And now I am going to have to say goodbye to Amanda because she is moving. Boo!

Amanda was asking me something. "Do you want to see a picture of my new house?" She was already getting it from her dressing table.

"Wow!" I said when I looked at the picture. It was about twice the size of Daddy's house. And his house is a mansion!

"It's really pretty inside. The front hallway is marble. Marble is really expensive, you know," said Amanda.

(Amanda was being snobby. So I ignored her.)

"And Granny and Grandpa live nearby. So I will get to see them a lot," continued Amanda. "But I still do not want to leave this house. I do not want to say goodbye to my friends, or my teacher, or my room, or the neighbourhood, or anything."

Amanda looked as if she was going to cry. I had to do something. Fast.

"Moving will not be so bad. Really. We just have to do a few things to make it easier," I said. "Do you have some paper and felt-tips? We will make a list."

Amanda went to her desk. She had paper of every colour in the rainbow, with felt-tips to match.

I picked pink paper and a purple pen. At the top of the paper, I wrote:

## THINGS TO DO BEFORE MOVING

Right away, we thought of three things to put on our list:

1. SPEND LOTS OF TIME TOGETHER AND DO EVERYTHING FUN AT LEAST ONCE
2. FIND A MOVING-DAY-GOOD-LUCK CHARM.
3. TAKE PICTURES OF SPECIAL PLACES.

I had one more idea. But I was not going to write it down. It would be a surprise. Anyway, I had to ask Daddy and Elizabeth first. But I was sure they would say yes.

In my head I wrote down:

4. HAVE A GOOD BYE PARTY!

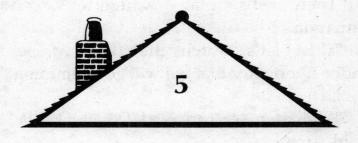

**5**

# Lovely Ladies

It was Sunday. I was back at Amanda's house. We had to do everything fun at least once.

"Let's play Lovely Ladies first," said Amanda.

"Okay," I replied. I play that game with Hannie and Nancy a lot. But Amanda was the one who started it.

I helped Amanda drag her trunk of dressing-up clothes out of her cupboard. (Her cupboard is almost as big as my whole room at the little house.)

"When we finish, let's play Snail!" I said.

"Then let's play Nintendo!" cried Amanda.

"Then let's watch the *Little Mermaid* video. And after that we will go swimming!" I said.

"And then we can read *Doctor Dolittle!*" said Amanda.

Amanda opened her trunk of clothes. If we wanted to do everything, we had to hurry. So I said, "One, two, three, go!"

"That is not how we start Lovely Ladies," said Amanda.

"It's how we start today," I said.

I was already pulling clothes out of Amanda's trunk. I pulled out a pink lace dress. I put it on. Only it was inside out. I grabbed shoes. One was yellow with a high heel. The other was blue with a low heel.

"Too bad. No time to change," I said, giggling.

Amanda grabbed a hat. She put it on backwards. She put on gloves. One was white. One was blue.

24

We piled on lots of clothes. Then we stood in front of the mirror. We looked so silly.

"Let's say everything together," I said. "And we have to say it fast."

You see, one of us always says, "Oh, I am a lovely, lovely lady."

Then the other one says, "Would you like to have some tea?"

Then the first one says, "Why, certainly. Lovely ladies must always have tea."

I counted to three again and we started together. We talked really fast. The words came out, "O-why-um-a-lolly-lolly!"

*Ding-dong!* We were laughing so hard, we almost did not hear the doorbell.

We ran downstairs. We still had on our *lolly-lolly* clothes. And we were still laughing. Amanda opened the door. It was Hannie. She looked cross.

"I thought you were playing with *me* this weekend, Karen. You always play with me when you stay at your daddy's house."

I stopped laughing. "Amanda's moving,"

I said. "I have to see her before she goes."

"You could have played with Amanda yesterday, and me today," complained Hannie.

"I see you every day at school," I said. "And you are not moving. So I will see you tomorrow."

"I may be going to school tomorrow. But I will not be talking to you!" said Hannie. She ran off in a huff.

I had made Hannie jealous. I was sorry about that. But Hannie had been cross with me before. We always make up.

Now I had to spend time with Amanda. Soon she would be moving.

"Where is your chalk?" I said. "It's time to play Snail!"

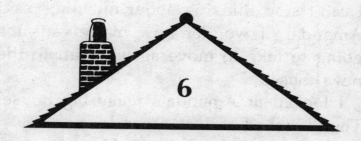

**6**

# The New Family

Amanda drew a huge spiral on the ground with the chalk. Then we both drew lines to make boxes.

"You can go first," I said. (I was trying extra hard to be nice.)

"Okay," said Amanda. She did not sound too excited. *Hop*. She landed in the first box. *Hop*. She landed in the second box. *Hop* . . .

"Oops. I stepped on a line. It's your turn," said Amanda.

"You were not really trying," I said. "That's no fun."

"That stupid Hannie upset me. And now I can't stop thinking about moving," said Amanda. "I wonder how many vans it's going to take to move all our stuff to the new house."

I looked at Amanda's really big house. Then I looked back at Amanda.

"At least a thousand!" I said.

"What if I leave something behind?" asked Amanda.

"Don't worry. I will send it to you," I said. "Hey! Have you told Priscilla she's moving?"

"Not yet," said Amanda. "I'll go and get her."

Amanda came back with Priscilla.

"Now, Priscilla, I have something important to tell you," said Amanda. "We are moving away to another house. What do you think of that?"

She held Priscilla's face up to her ear so she could hear her answer.

"Oh, good," said Amanda. "Priscilla thinks it will be fun to move. She says there will be new grass to smell. And new cats to play with. And she won't ever, ever have her tail hurt by that naughty Pat."

(Pat is Hannie's kitten. Once she pounced on Priscilla's tail. Amanda got really cross.)

"You know, I think Priscilla is right," continued Amanda. "Moving *will* be fun. I'll get a brand-new room. And the pool at the new house is so, so beautiful. It's shaped like a giant flower."

"I think Priscilla is right, too. Moving can be really fun!" I said.

What I wanted to say was, "Especially when you get to have a goodbye party planned by *me* with lots of people and food and presents." Ooh! I wanted to say it so, so much. But I didn't. That is because I am good at keeping surprises.

"Karen!" called Mrs Delaney. "Kristy just called. Your family would like you to come home now."

I said goodbye to Amanda. But not too big a goodbye. I had to save my really big goodbye for moving day.

While I was walking home, I started wondering who would move into the Delaneys' house when they were gone.

Oh, no! I thought. What if a whole family of *boys* moves in? Yuck.

Or maybe just two really old people. I like old people. But I already have lots of grandparents.

Or maybe it will be a lot of burglars. Would they wear masks all the time, I wondered.

Or maybe it would be a family of lion tamers. Scary! They would go to the supermarket one day to buy all the meat in the shop for their hungry lions. Then they would get stuck in traffic on the way home. The lions would get bored waiting for them. And they would come out, cross the street, and walk up to our house . . . yikes!

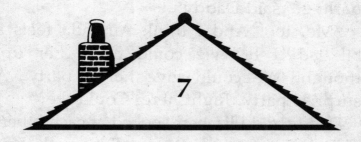

# Invitations

Hurray! Andrew and I got to stay at the big house for Sunday night dinner. That was because Mummy and Seth had gone to the country. They were going to pick up Andrew and me later.

Daddy and Elizabeth were in the kitchen getting dinner ready. It was the perfect time to ask them about the goodbye party for Amanda.

"Daddy, did you know that Amanda Delaney is moving away?" I asked.

"Yes. I spoke to Mr Delaney earlier in the

week. I'm sorry your friend is leaving, darling," said Daddy.

"Me, too. And I think Amanda feels a bit sad. I bet we could cheer her up, though. We could give her a party. A surprise party. Right here. Could we?"

Daddy and Elizabeth looked at each other. They have a special way of talking with their eyes.

Finally Elizabeth said, "I think it's a wonderful idea."

"I think so, too," said Daddy. "A party will make Amanda feel very special."

"Wow! Thank you!" I said. "I've never given a goodbye party before. I want to invite lots of people. And I want it to be a happy party, not a sad one."

"Games are happy," said Elizabeth. "Maybe you could play Pin the Tail on the Donkey."

"Oh, yes! And we could have prizes. We could have little whistles, and Super Stickers, and ruby rings!"

"What about decorations?" asked Daddy.

"Balloons and streamers," I said. "*Lots* of streamers." Planning parties is great fun!

"You will need a cake," said Elizabeth. "I can help you bake it."

"We can write *Goodbye, Amanda* on it," I said. "No. That would be too sad."

"Let's think, then," said Daddy. "What do you want to say to a friend who is leaving?"

"I know!" I said. "I will write *Good luck, Amanda!*"

"Terrific!" said Daddy. "Now, do you want to give Amanda a present?"

"Yes," I said. "I want it to be something really special. Something that will always remind Amanda of her friends in Stoneybrook. I need to think about it for a while."

"Karen, dinner is almost ready now," said Elizabeth. "Will you bring these plates out to the table, please? We'll talk more about your party later on."

After dinner I went upstairs and made

out my invitation list. First I wrote the names of everyone at the big house: Watson, Elizabeth, Kristy, David Michael, Charlie, Sam, Emily Michelle, Nannie, Andrew, KAREN! (I was not inviting Shannon and Boo-Boo.)

I left spaces for three of Amanda's friends from school. Amanda doesn't go to my school. She goes to Stoneybrook Day School. But Mrs Delaney could give me their names.

Next I wrote Maria Kilbourne. She's eight and lives right next door to Amanda.

Then I wrote Nancy Dawes. She does not know Amanda very well. But she is my best friend and she loves parties.

What about Hannie? I did not know whether to invite her. First of all, she did not like Amanda one bit. Second of all, she was cross with me. And I was a little bit cross with her, too.

But she is still my best friend, I thought. And if I don't invite her, she will feel left out. Then she will be more cross than ever.

I added Hannie's name to the list. If she doesn't want to come, she doesn't have to, I decided.

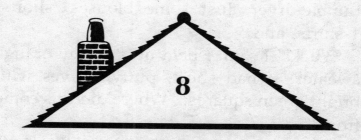

# The Mummy Blanket

It was Tuesday. Mummy dropped me off at Amanda's house again after school. I had promised to help Amanda clear out her room. She was moving in eight days.

"I don't know where to start," said Amanda.

I looked around her room. Shelves. Toy chest. Cupboard. Drawers . . .

"Let's find out what's in Drawer Number One!" I said. I was acting like a game show host. "Oooh! Maybe there will be a tumble-dryer."

Amanda opened the top drawer. No tumble-dryer. Just some blouses, shorts, T-shirts, and . . .

"Yuck!" I said. I held up an itchy orange sweater. It had short, puffy sleeves with bright green squares. "Where did this come from?"

"My Aunt Gayle gave it to me. I think she hates me," said Amanda, taking the sweater.

"You're not going to keep it, are you?" I asked.

Amanda had a funny look in her eye. "I was going to give it to you for your birthday, but . . ."

"Ugh, gross!" I said. I grabbed the sweater and threw it into the giveaway box Mrs Delaney had put in Amanda's room.

Drawer Number Two had pyjamas, T-shirts, marbles, and a little pink teddy bear that smelled nice.

"This is called a sachet. My grandma gave it to me," explained Amanda. "Oh, look. Here's a nightie from when I was a tiny, little baby."

I could hardly believe Amanda was ever that small. She folded the nightie and put it back into her drawer.

"Aren't you going to give it away?" I asked.

"No. I still like it," said Amanda. "Maybe I will let one of my dolls wear it."

Drawer Number Three was filled mostly with socks. But we found a bag of seashells, one small black doll's shoe, a notebook that said "Top Secret" (Amanda would not let me look in it), an old peppermint stick, and right in the corner, a small white box tied with string.

"What's in it?" I asked. "A diamond ring?"

"I don't know," said Amanda. She untied the string. Inside the box was a four-leaf-clover key-ring.

"I remember this!" said Amanda. "I bought it at a fair last year. And right after I got it, I won a teddy bear."

"That means it's lucky. It could be your good-luck-moving charm," I said.

"That's right," said Amanda. She put the key-ring in her pocket.

We had finished with the drawers, so we started on the toy box. Amanda had a zillion toys. She had about seventeen Barbie and Ken dolls. Two of them were tied together at the wrist with red ribbon.

"They're married," explained Amanda.

I was busy winding up an old jack-in-the-box. It played, "Here We Go Round the Mulberry Bush". When it popped open we both jumped about ten feet.

We laughed, but then Amanda threw it in the giveaway box. "That clown always scared me," she said.

We found a wooden lady you could open up. Inside was another, smaller lady. When you opened *her* up, there was an even smaller lady. I kept opening them until I got to the last teeny, tiny lady.

"You can have it if you want," said Amanda.

"Thanks," I said. I really liked it. I

carefully put all the little ladies back where they belonged.

Amanda was holding a ragged piece of blue cloth to her cheek.

"Ugh, what's that?" I asked.

"Don't say anything bad about it," said Amanda. "This is all that is left of my Mummy Blanket. I used to sleep with it when I was little. I am definitely taking it with me."

"I would definitely take Tickly, too," I agreed.

Suddenly we both remembered something. We remembered why we were clearing out Amanda's room.

Amanda was *really* moving.

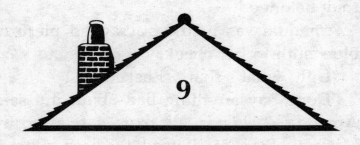

# Pictures

"I've got it! I've got the camera," I said.

It was Thursday afternoon. I was back at Amanda's house. Six more days to moving day.

Mummy and I had stopped at Daddy's house first. He said I could borrow his really good camera because Mr Delaney's was broken. Daddy's camera is easy to use. All you have to do is press one button.

"I'll take lots of pictures," I said. "I will give them to you as soon as they are developed."

"Let's take pictures of my room first," said Amanda.

It was probably the last time I would see Amanda's room the way it was. The next time, it would be all packed up.

I looked at her thick pink carpet and her great big bed with the white lace canopy. On her bedside table was a Peter Rabbit lamp with a pink shade that matched the carpet. There was a picture window with a seat and lots of pretty cushions. The room was so big, I had to take a few pictures to get everything in.

*Click! Click! Click!*

"Can I take some pictures, too?" asked Amanda.

"Okay. Just be careful," I said. I showed Amanda how the camera worked.

We took turns taking pictures of every room in the house — all the bedrooms (I think there were six), the playroom (toys were *everywhere*), her mother's dressing room (can you believe she has a dressing room?), the kitchen (with its outer-space gadgets), the living room (all white), the library (very fancy), the hall with the fish fountain (I asked Amanda to stand next to it on her tip-toes and pretend she was spitting with the fish, but she said no), and all four bathrooms — white, blue, pink, and green with matching soaps and towels.

It was a good thing I had lots of film.

*Click! Click! Click! Click!*

Amanda went back to her room. She got a book and a piece of chalk. Then we went outside.

Amanda took her book and sat under her favourite tree. That's where she liked to read. I took a picture. *Click!*

We drew Snail boxes on the ground. I took a picture of Amanda hopping into one. *Click!*

I took pictures of the two tennis courts. *Click! Click!*

And Amanda took a picture of me pretending I was going to dive into the pool with my clothes on. *Click!*

Then Mrs Delaney came outside.

"Mummy, will you please take some pictures of us together?" asked Amanda.

"Of course," said Mrs Delaney.

She took some more pictures of us at the pool and two in front of the house. Then I had an idea.

"Come on!" I said to Amanda. We went to her room and put on our dressing-up hats. I asked Mrs Delaney if we could take a picture in her dressing room. The room has a three-sided mirror. If you stand in front of it just right, you can see yourself over and over and over again.

Amanda and I put on our hats. We smiled our loveliest Lovely Lady smiles. We stood in just the right spot. It looked like we went on for ever and ever.

*Click!*

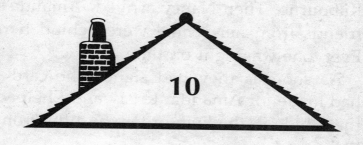

# Surprise!

"Party! Party! We're going to have a party!" I sang. It was Saturday. I was at the big house. It was almost time for Amanda's goodbye party.

This is what I was wearing: my shiny black party shoes, white trousers, a purple-and-white-striped T-shirt, and my favourite purple hair ribbon.

There were balloons everywhere. And *lots* of coloured streamers, just like I wanted.

"Hello! Anyone home?" called a voice.

I went to the back door. Daddy and

Elizabeth were saying hello to Maria Kilbourne. Then Nancy arrived. Amanda's friends from her school were behind her. Everyone was right on time.

As soon as they had signed the card I had made for Amanda, Kristy and I helped them hide in the living room and the front hall.

My guests were having so much fun. I wished Hannie had come. But she said she did not want to.

"Is everyone ready?" I asked.

The guests all said yes. I looked around to make sure you could not see anyone. That's when I saw Andrew's head sticking up from behind a table. I moved a vase in front of him.

Then I phoned Amanda. Her mummy and daddy knew all about the party. They made sure Amanda would be at home when I phoned.

"Hi, it's Karen," I said into the phone. "Guess what! I got the photos back. Come over and see them."

I hung up and ran to the window. In about half a minute I saw Amanda heading for our house.

"Okay, everybody. Quiet!" I said. (I felt really important.)

*Ding-dong!* I opened the door for Amanda and . . .

"Surprise!" everyone shouted.

"Oh, wow!" said Amanda. "I can't believe it! This is great!" Amanda really looked surprised. And happy!

"Who wants to have a relay race?" asked Kristy.

We all did. We went into the back garden to play. Kristy is really good at organizing games. I was glad when Amanda's team won, especially since I was in it. Kristy gave out the prizes. We all got whistles.

Then we played musical rug. This is how: Kristy put a bath mat in the garden. Sam played a Michael Jackson tape. We walked around in a circle and made sure we crossed the mat. Whoever was on the mat when the music stopped was out.

You know what? The music stopped the minute I stepped on the mat. Boo! (Sam promised he did not do it on purpose. But I don't believe him.)

We played Pin the Tail on the Donkey. Andrew won and got a page of Super Stickers. I was glad.

Then everyone lined up to have a picture taken with Amanda. Kristy used Elizabeth's Polaroid camera so we could see the pictures straight away. She took two photos of each of us. When everyone had had their picture taken, Elizabeth made an announcement.

"It's time for cake and ice cream. Everyone come to the table, please," she said.

The cake was white with pink candles and pink writing that said, *Good luck, Amanda!*

"It's not your birthday, but you can make a wish anyway because you are moving," I said.

Amanda closed her eyes. Her face was glowing in the candles. "I wish that

everyone here will stay my friend after I move."

Then — *whoosh!* — she blew out the candles.

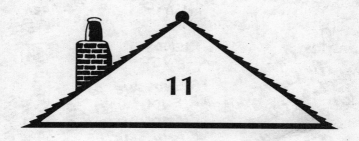

# Friends 4-Ever

First I ate some ice cream. Then I ate some cake. Then I ate more ice cream. Then more cake. Yum!

When I had finished, Elizabeth whispered to me, "I think this would be a good time to give Amanda her presents."

Oh, goody! The presents were hidden in the cloakroom. I ran and got them.

First Amanda opened the giant card I had made. Inside in really big letters I had written, *Friends 4-Ever.* Then everyone had written nice things and funny things, too:

Dear Amanda,
Good luck in your new house.
Nancy

ANDREW

Here's a few lines to remember me by
Sam

Dear Amanda,
Be nice to your new baby-sitters. We'll miss you!
Love
Kristy

FRIENDS 4-EVER

FRIENDS WE R
FRIENDS WE'LL B.
FRIENDS 4-EVER,
U AND ME!
LOVE,
KAREN

GOOD LUCK AMANDA, WATSON AND ELIZABETH BREWER

Dot-blot-forget-me-not
your friend,
Maria

"This is great! Thank you, everybody," said Amanda.

If Amanda thought the card was great, wait till she saw her other present. It had taken me a long time to decide what to give Amanda. I hoped she would like it.

Amanda was taking off the paper really carefully. I bet she wanted to save it. It was pink, with balloons and confetti. And I had written *Goodbye!*, *Good luck!* and *Surprise!* all over it.

You should have seen Amanda's face

54

when she opened the box. She almost cried.

This was the gift: It was a photograph album. On the front of it I had written, *Amanda's House.* Inside I had put all the pictures we had taken of Amanda and me and her house. I had written what everything was under each picture, so Amanda would always remember.

"I love my present so much, Karen. Thank you!" said Amanda. She even gave me a kiss.

Everyone wanted to see the album. So we passed it around. I heard the guests saying things like, "Wow!" and, "What a good idea!" I felt really proud.

"If I ever move away, will you make an album like that for me?" said Nancy. I told her I would, but that she had better not move away.

It was getting pretty late. People had to leave.

"This was a super party," said Maria. "Thanks for inviting me."

"Wait! Don't forget your photos!" I said.

I handed everyone their Polaroid picture on the way out.

Then just me and Amanda and my big-house family were left.

"Here is one more present," I said. I handed Amanda the extra set of photos Kristy had taken. I explained that there were a few pages left at the end of the album. "You could put these in the album. Then if you miss anyone, you could just look at their picture."

"Thanks a lot, Karen," said Amanda. "I can't believe I'm moving on Wednesday. It's so soon!"

"We hope you will come and visit us," said Elizabeth.

"And we can drive Karen over to visit you sometimes, too," said Daddy.

"Friends forever!" I said.

"I'd better go home now," said Amanda. "Thank you all so, so much for this party. It was the greatest!"

Amanda ran out the door. She looked happy and sad all at the same time.

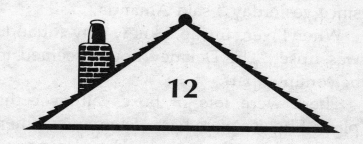

# Coming Apart

Tuesday was packing day at the Delaneys'.

"See you later, alligator," said Mummy when she dropped me off. I waved and ran up the drive.

Maybe I should say "See you later, alligator" to Amanda when she moved. That was better than goodbye. It meant I would see her again.

Amanda was waiting for me at the door. She looked upset and a little scared.

"The removal men have been packing since yesterday," said Amanda.

When I went inside, I knew why Amanda was upset. The Delaney house seemed to be coming apart.

There were lots of boxes all over the place. Shelves were bare. The removal men were pushing things around and covering them up.

Even the fish fountain looked sad. The fish was standing on its tail. But it was not spitting any more. Someone had turned it off.

"Girls, the removal men are working down here now," said Mrs Delaney. "Why don't you go upstairs and play?"

We started to go upstairs. On the way, we passed the library. I peeked in. There used to be so many books. Now they were all gone. Suddenly I thought of something funny.

"Remember when we took the books off the shelves and tried to put them back in alphabetical order?" I said.

58

"Mummy and Daddy got so angry!" said Amanda. "They said the books were in a very special order and it would take them days to put them back."

"We were only trying to help," I said, giggling.

"And remember what we did to the basement when Mummy asked me to put soap in the washing-machine?" said Amanda.

"I remember," I said. "You put some soap in. But I didn't know you'd put it in, so I put in some more!"

"And then when we were upstairs, Mummy called, 'A-*man*-da!' And we ran downstairs and —"

"There were soapsuds *everywhere*!" I said.

On the first floor, things looked even weirder. The house was so empty that when I talked, I could hear an echo. I headed for the playroom.

"Don't bother," said Amanda.

I saw why. There was nothing to play

with. The room was bare. It was not the playroom any more. It was the nothing room.

"Let's just go to my room," said Amanda.

It was filled with boxes. There were no more pretty cushions. There were no pictures on the walls.

"Where's Priscilla?" I asked.

"She's under the bed. She won't come out," said Amanda.

I got down on the floor. "Here, kitty, kitty!" I said. I really wanted Priscilla to come out. We needed her company. But she would not budge.

"I don't blame you," I whispered.

*Knock-knock.* It was Mrs Delaney. She had a tray of biscuits and milk for us. Amanda and I did not talk much while we ate.

"I've still got paper and felt-tips," said Amanda when we had finished eating. "We could draw pictures."

We tried to draw what Amanda's house looked like last Tuesday afternoon. It was hard to remember.

Then Mummy came to pick me up. I cried the whole way home. I could not believe that tomorrow, Amanda Delaney was moving.

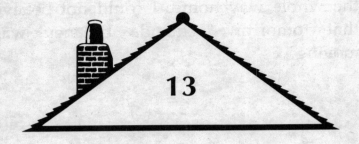

# Moving Day

This is it, I thought, as Mummy pulled up at the Delaneys' house. It was Wednesday. Moving day.

Lots of kids from the neighbourhood were standing outside the house. They were watching the removal men put things into vans. (There were not a thousand vans, like I had said there would be. There were just three.)

At first, I did not see Amanda. Then she ran out of the house.

"Karen! They're moving my bedroom furniture right this minute," she moaned.

The removal men came out behind her. They were carrying crates filled with Amanda's things. Her Peter Rabbit lamp was sticking out of one of them.

"I don't want them to hurt Peter," said Amanda.

"Don't worry. They won't. And look, he's next to your teddy bear. They can talk all the way to the new house."

I was trying to cheer Amanda up. But it was not working. She looked very worried. Then she started crying.

So I held hands with her. We stayed like that, without saying a word, until the removal men finished putting her things in the van. Then we heard a voice from the back garden.

"Here, kitty, kitty! Here, kitty, kitty!" It was Mrs Delaney. Amanda dried her eyes and we went around the back to see what was going on.

Priscilla was racing around the garden.

Amanda's mummy was running after her. She was trying to catch Priscilla to put her in her travelling basket.

Amanda's mother went this way. "Here, kitty!" she called. Priscilla went that way.

Amanda's mother went that way. "Here, kitty!" she called. Priscilla went the other way.

We were all laughing and trying to help Mrs Delaney catch Priscilla when Mr Delaney came clomping out of the back door.

*"Me-ow!"* Priscilla jumped into Amanda's arms. I think Mr Delaney had scared her. You should have seen him!

He usually wears a suit and tie, and carries a briefcase. (That is because he's a lawyer.) Now he was wearing ordinary trousers and a T-shirt. He was also wearing flippers, a diving mask, and an inflatable duck rubber ring.

"It seems they forgot to pack our pool things, dear," said Mr Delaney to Mrs Delaney. "Anyone for a swim?" he added with a wink.

64

One of the removal men came around the back.

"We've just about finished loading the vans, Mr and Mrs Delaney," he said. "Would you like to check the house before we pull out?"

We carried Priscilla inside and put her in her cat basket. The removal men were lugging out one last bookcase.

It was too sad inside. The house was completely empty.

Amanda carried Priscilla to the car. It was time for her to go.

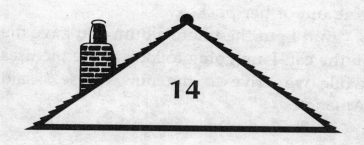

# Goodbye, Amanda!

The vans started creeping down the drive. Mr and Mrs Delaney were waiting in their car.

"Please say goodbye to your friends now," Mrs Delaney called.

"I'll be there in a minute, Mummy," said Amanda. Lots of kids from the neighbourhood had come to say goodbye to Amanda and her little brother, Max.

"Do you have your good-luck-moving charm?" I asked.

Amanda pulled the four-leaf-clover key ring out of her pocket.

"And I put the photo album you gave me in the car. I am going to look at the pictures while we drive to the new house," said Amanda.

"We'll write to each other, right?" I asked.

"I'll write to you!" said Amanda.

"And I will write to you, too," I said.

Then guess who came running over. It was Hannie! She looked as if she wanted to make up.

"Hi, everybody," she said.

"Hi," I said.

"Hi," said Amanda.

"I just wanted to say, Amanda, that I am sorry I didn't come to your party. And I wanted to say goodbye and good luck and everything."

"Thanks," said Amanda. "I wanted to say goodbye to you, too."

"Amanda! Max! In the car, please," called Mr Delaney.

I could not think of anything else to say. Neither could Amanda. But I could see she did not want to go yet. And I did not want her to.

So we just stood around. Then Mr Delaney honked his car horn twice. Max was already in the back seat.

"Well, I suppose I'd better go now," said Amanda.

"I suppose so," I said. Amanda and I gave each other a hug. (Hannie took a few little steps back. Saying goodbye to Amanda was one thing. Hugging her was another.)

Amanda started walking backwards to the car.

"So we're really going to write, aren't we? And will you phone me sometimes, too?" said Amanda.

"Yup. And you phone me," I said.

She was still walking backwards.

"Give Priscilla a pat for me," I said.

"I will," said Amanda. "Goodbye!"

"Goodbye, Amanda!" I called.

I did not get the chance to say, "See you

later, alligator." Amanda turned, ran to the car, and climbed in before I had the chance.

We waved to each other while the car pulled out of the driveway.

We kept waving while it rolled down the street.

I was still waving when the car turned the corner.

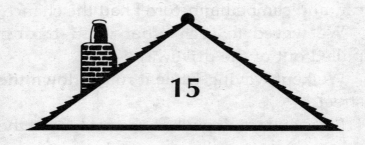

# Vampires?

"The Delaney house looks really lonely now," I said.

Nancy and I were in the school playground waiting for Hannie to arrive. It was a Wednesday morning. Amanda had moved away a whole week ago.

"Of course it looks lonely," said Nancy. "A house needs people in it."

"Well, I found out that a family is going to move in soon. But I don't know when. And I don't know what kind of family it's going to be yet," I told Nancy.

We saw Hannie getting out of her mummy's car. She ran over to us.

"Hi!" she said. "What are you talking about?"

(The Three Musketeers were together again. I was so, so happy.)

"We were talking about the Delaney house," I said. "Who do you think is going to move in?"

"Very, very rich people," said Hannie. "Maybe they will be famous, too."

"Maybe they will be TV stars. Or film stars!" I said.

"I hope not," said Hannie. "Then they might be snobby, just like Aman —"

I gave Hannie my you'd-better-not-or-I'll-be-really-cross look. I did not want to start fighting all over again.

"I think Hannie was going to say, 'They might be snobby like a man she once knew.' Right, Hannie?" said Nancy.

"Um, right," said Hannie. "You know what I think? I think a family of vampires is packing their bags right now."

"They will have to bring their pet bats along with them," I said. I started flapping my arms like they were bat wings.

"Most of the time, they will act like a normal family," said Nancy.

"Except on Hallowe'en," said Hannie. "They will not even have to wear costumes!"

"And when Mr Tastee's ice-cream van comes, you know what flavour the vampire children will ask for?" I said.

"What?" said Nancy and Hannie.

"They will ask for vein-illa!" I said, laughing. (I had read a joke like that in a book once.)

Suddenly I stopped laughing. In a low and eerie voice, I said, "What if it's witches? What if Morbidda Destiny's relatives move in?" (Morbidda Destiny is the witch who lives next door to Daddy's house. Daddy thinks she is just a nice lady. But I know better.)

"Ooh, scary," said Nancy.

"Ooh, really scary!" said Hannie.

"Ooh, really, really scary!" I said. And, you know what? I meant it.

I was glad when the school bell rang.

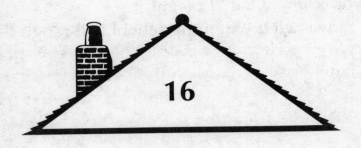

# New Neighbours

"**H**ave you heard from Amanda?" asked Kristy.

"Not yet," I replied. "But I know I will soon."

It was Friday night at the big house. We were in the kitchen eating my favourite dinner: hamburgers, mashed potatoes, and peas and carrots. (I like to mush the peas and carrots into the mashed potatoes. It makes the potatoes look pretty.)

*Ring! Ring!* Kristy jumped up to answer the phone.

"It's for you, Karen," she called. "It's Hannie."

I love it when it's for me! I picked up the phone. Hannie had big news. The new family was moving in the next day.

"Whoever sees the removal van first has to phone the other," I said. "We will visit the neighbours together."

Hannie said okay. Then we hung up. I was really excited. (I was a little scared, too. What if Morbidda Destiny's relatives really did move in? That was one reason I wanted to visit the new neighbours with Hannie.)

When I got back to the table, I told everyone the news.

"Did Hannie say what kind of family it's going to be?" asked Charlie.

"I hope it's a family of cute girls!" said Sam.

That made me feel really good. Sam wanted more girls like me! I sat up tall in my chair.

Sam noticed. "I did not mean *little* girls," he said. "I meant grown-up high-school girls."

*Boo.* I should have known.

"Maybe there will be some boys our age," said Charlie. "I would like that, too."

"I hope there will be a boy who is almost eight, like me. And I hope he is good at softball," said David Michael.

"Speaking on behalf of The Babysitters Club," said Kristy, "I hope the family will have lots of babies and little children. That way we will have a new babysitting job."

"*A girl! A girl! A girl! I want there to be a girl!*" I sang.

After dinner, I helped Nannie put Emily to bed. (At New Year  I had made a special promise to do one nice thing a day. Most of the time I forgot. But sometimes, like tonight, I remembered.)

"Who do you hope the new neighbours will be?" I asked Nannie.

"Oh, I don't know," said Nannie. "I will be happy if they are young or old or boys or girls."

Or space creatures! I thought. But I did not say it.

That night when I went to sleep, I dreamed a cat family moved into the Delaney house. The cats were the size of people. One was a seven-year-old girl. Her name was Muffy.

"Come on. I'll show you around Stoneybrook Academy," I said to Muffy in my dream. "That will be your new school."

We started walking into school, but we were blinded by a really bright light. We had to shut our eyes tight.

I made myself open my eyes. I sat up. Bright sun was shining through my window. It was morning!

"Wake up, Moosie and Tickly," I said. "Today is the day I meet our new neighbours!"

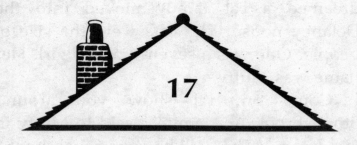

# Waiting and Waiting

Waiting, waiting, waiting. It was the longest Saturday morning in history.

First of all, I felt as if I was still dreaming. Everywhere I looked I saw cats. There was one on Emily Michelle's bib. There were cats on the cartoons David Michael was watching on TV. And of course, there was our real cat, Boo-Boo. He was curled up next to Shannon.

What if a family of cats really did move in? And what if they were mean, like Boo-Boo? No, that is not possible, I thought.

But it was possible that a horrible family of real people could move in. And it was definitely possible for Morbidda Destiny's relatives to come. Witches like to stick together.

I was glad when Elizabeth called, "Come and have some breakfast, Karen."

I could hardly eat anything, though. I was too excited.

I tried watching cartoons with David Michael. But I do not like cartoons very much. (I like to watch *Mister Ed*, the show about the talking horse. But it was not on.)

I looked out of the window. No removal vans yet.

"Want to play a game?" asked Andrew. "We could play draughts."

"All right," I said. Maybe that would help take my mind off the new neighbours.

We played for an hour. Every time it was Andrew's turn, I jumped up and went to the window. That meant I jumped up about thirteen times. There were still no vans.

I played with Emily for another whole

hour. I made sure we were sitting near a window, so I would not have to keep jumping up.

We pretended we were having a little tea party.

> *"Here's a cup and here's a cup*
> *And here's a pot of tea.*
> *Pour a cup and pour a cup*
> *And have some tea with me."*

We started to play Pat-a-Cake next. That's when I saw it! A removal van was pulling into the driveway.

I ran as fast as I could to phone Hannie. She promised to come over right away.

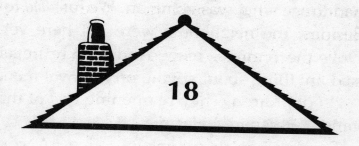

# 18

# The Spies

**H**annie was on our front doorstep in a flash.

"I'm going outside to play, Daddy!" I called. (I did not tell Daddy what we were going to do. He would not be too happy if he knew.)

"We have to see *every*thing!" I said to Hannie. "We have to see all the people and their furniture. As much as we can."

We hid behind a bush in the front garden. If Daddy found out what I was doing, he would be cross. There is a rule at the big house: no spying on neighbours. But we had to see what was going on. We just *had* to. Besides, the neighbours were not here yet. Only the removal men. And Daddy never said anything about spying on removal men.

"Look, Karen! They're opening one of the vans," whispered Hannie.

Guess what they took out first. A cot. Boo. That meant there was a baby. Maybe it was a family of babies. Triplets. Or quintuplets. At least Kristy would happy.

They took out a sofa. Bookcases. Chairs. No clues there.

"Oh, no! Do you see what I see?" I asked Hannie.

Hannie only nodded. She was too scared to talk. That is because the removal men were taking out a big, long broom. It looked as if Morbidda Destiny's relatives were moving in after all.

When one van was empty, the removal men opened the next. Television. Lamps. Lawn mower. Bicycle. Yikes! It was a *boy's* bicycle.

Babies. Witches. Boys.

"Hannie, we're in trouble," I said.

Then I saw a car turning into the driveway.

"They're he-ere!" I whispered loudly.

The car pulled up, then stopped. First a man and a woman got out. The woman opened the back door. She leaned into the car and started fumbling around. When she came out, she was holding a baby.

Next a boy climbed out. He looked like he was about ten.

Then I saw a foot. It was in trainers. Then a leg. It was wearing shorts. Boy or girl?

"A girl! There's a girl!" cried Hannie.

She looked as if she was seven, just like us.

We waited a little longer to make sure no one else came out of the car. What a relief. No witches, or vampires, or cats, or lion tamers. Just an ordinary family, and they even had a girl.

"Maybe we should go over and say hi," I suggested.

"Maybe," said Hannie.

But neither of us got up. We watched a little longer. Then I realized we were spying on neighbours, not removal men. And I do not like to disobey rules *too* much.

"Let's go," I said.

I climbed out from behind the bush. I brushed off a few leaves.

"How do I look?" (I wanted to make a good first impression.)

"You look okay," said Hannie. "How do I look?"

"Okay," I said.

We crossed the street. I walked straight up to the new girl.

"Hi, I'm Karen," I said.

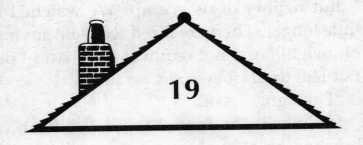

# 19

# Melody

"My name's Melody," said the new girl.

"That's a pretty name," I told her.

"Thanks. Karen and Hannie are nice names, too," said Melody.

I liked Melody already. And I could tell Hannie did, too. What a relief! I was afraid that I would like Melody, and Hannie would not. Or that Hannie would like her and *I* would not. Or that neither of us would like her. But the three of us were going to get along fine. I could tell.

"We're both seven," said Hannie. "How old are you?"

Melody said she was just seven. (That was good.) She said she liked pets. (Even better.) And she liked dressing up. (Perfect!) We would have to introduce her to Boo-Boo (maybe) and to Shannon and to Pat the cat. And we would teach her Lovely Ladies.

Melody introduced us to her mummy and daddy, her brother, Bill (he's nine), and her baby sister, Skylar.

"Where do you live?" asked Melody.

"I live two houses away," said Hannie. "And I have a brother. He's nine. His name is Linnie. I have a little sister, too. She's two. Her name is Sari."

"I live over there, across the street," I said. I pointed to Daddy's house. I told her about everybody who lived there. (I did not tell her about Mummy's house. I would save that for another time.)

"Are you going to go to Stoneybrook

Academy? That's where we go," said Hannie.

"No. I'm going to go to Stoneybrook Day School," said Melody.

"That's where Amanda went. She's the girl who used to live here," I explained. "But going to different schools did not matter. We played together a lot anyway."

Secretly I was glad Melody was going to Stoneybrook Day School. I liked her. But Hannie and Nancy and I were the Three Musketeers. And if Melody went to our school and we all got along really well, we might have to become the Four Musketeers. And who had ever heard of that?

"Want to take a walk with us?" I asked. "We could show you around the neighbourhood."

"Okay. I just have to ask my mummy and daddy," Melody replied.

"I hope they say yes. We will show you the witch's house!" I said.

I did not want to scare Melody. But

I wanted her to know that living in Stoneybrook — especially with me and Hannie for neighbours — was going to be pretty exciting.

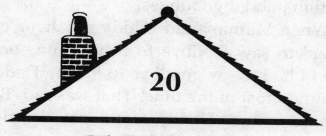

# 20

# Old Friends New Friends

"Guess what, Moosie!" I said. "There's a new girl in the neighbourhood. And she is really nice. Her name is Melody."

I was up in my room. Hannie and I had shown Melody all around the neighbourhood. She thought it was really nice. Especially Morbidda Destiny's house. She said there were not any witches where she came from.

Then Melody's mummy wanted her to help with Skylar. And Hannie had to go shopping with her family. But that was okay. I had some thinking to do. I needed to think about goodbyes.

When Mummy and Daddy got divorced, I had to say goodbye to being a one-one. And I had to say goodbye to having Daddy around most of the time. That was sad. But Mummy and Daddy each got married again, and I got *two* families. I love them so much.

When my goldfish, Crystal Light, died, I had to say goodbye. And I was angry and sad at the same time. But then I got Crystal Light the Second. And she is a really great fish.

Before that, Louie, David Michael's collie, died. When we said goodbye to him, we were very sad. But then we got Shannon, David Michael's new puppy. She isn't Louie. But we love her.

And two weeks ago, I had to say goodbye to my friend Amanda. But now Melody is here. And we are going to be friends.

"So, Moosie," I said, "sometimes you have to say goodbye to people and pets and things. And that is sad. But other ones come along. They do not take the *place* of the ones you lost. But they make you feel a lot, lot better."

"Karen! You've got a letter!" It was Kristy. Wow! I hardly ever get any post. I raced downstairs.

"Where is it? Where is my post?" I asked.

Kristy handed me a letter. It was from Amanda! On the back was a flower. Under the flower was written, FORGET ME NOT!

I ran back upstairs so I could read the letter to Moosie. And I took the little wooden ladies Amanda had given me. I lined them up so they could listen, too.

Here is what the letter said:

Dear Karen,
  Hi! How are you? I am fine.
  My new house is so, so beautiful! I think I am going to like living here. There's a girl across the street who's

almost nine, like me. She's really nice.
Her name is Aggie.

I looked at my album this morning.
Some of the pictures are really funny.
I miss you.

Write to me soon.

Amanda

"Look at that, Moosie!" I exclaimed. "I had to say goodbye to Amanda, but now I have her letter."

That is a good thing, I thought. Even when you have to say goodbye to someone, they can still be with you. You could have a letter, or pictures, or special memories.

I wrote an answer to Amanda right away. On the back of the envelope I drew a heart. Inside the heart I wrote, U R 2 NICE 2 BE 4-GOTTEN!

"I hope you heard everything I said to you about goodbyes, Moosie. Because I have to say goodbye to you now. But don't worry. I'm only going to the corner. I will be back very soon."

I gave Moosie a big kiss.

Then I went outside to post my letter to Amanda. I hoped I would see Melody on the way.

# GREEN WATCH by Anthony Masters

## BATTLE FOR THE BADGERS
Tim's been sent to stay with his weird Uncle Seb and his two kids, Flower and Brian, who run Green Watch – an environmental pressure group. At first Tim thinks they're a bunch of cranks – but soon he finds himself battling to save badgers from extermination . . .

## SAD SONG OF THE WHALE
Tim leaps at the chance to join Green Watch on an anti-whaling expedition. But soon, he and the other members of Green Watch, find themselves shipwrecked and fighting for their lives . . .

## DOLPHIN'S REVENGE
The members of Green Watch are convinced that Sam Jefferson is mistreating his dolphins – but how can they prove it? Not only that, but they must save Loner, a wild dolphin, from captivity . . .

## MONSTERS ON THE BEACH
The Green Watch team is called to investigate a suspected radiation leak. Teddy McCormack claims to have seen mutated crabs and sea-plants, but there's no proof, and Green Watch don't know whether he's crazy or there's been a cover-up . . .

## GORILLA MOUNTAIN
Tim, Brian and Flower fly to Africa to meet the Bests, who are protecting gorillas from poachers. But they are ambushed and Alison Best is kidnapped. It is up to them to rescue her *and* save the gorillas . . .

## SPIRIT OF THE CONDOR
Green Watch has gone to California on a surfing holiday – but not for long! Someone is trying to kill the Californian Condor, the bird cherished by an Indian tribe – the Daiku – and without which the tribe will die. Green Watch must struggle to save both the Condor and the Daiku . . .

# THE BABYSITTERS CLUB

Need a babysitter? Then call the Babysitters Club. Kristy Thomas and her friends are all experienced sitters. They can tackle any job from rampaging toddlers to a pandemonium of pets. To find out all about them, read on!

No 1: **Kristy's Great Idea**
No 2: **Claudia and the Phantom Phone Calls**
No 3: **The Truth About Stacey**
No 4: **Mary Anne Saves The Day**
No 5: **Dawn and the Impossible Three**
No 6: **Kristy's Big Day**
No 7: **Claudia and Mean Janine**
No 8: **Boy-Crazy Stacey**
No 9: **The Ghost at Dawn's House**
No 10: **Logan Likes Mary Anne!**
No 11: **Kristy and the Snobs**
No 12: **Claudia and the New Girl**
No 13: **Goodbye Stacey, Goodbye**
No 14: **Hello, Mallory**
No 15: **Little Miss Stoneybrook . . . and Dawn**
No 16: **Jessi's Secret Language**
No 17: **Mary Anne's Bad-Luck Mystery**
No 18: **Stacey's Mistake**
No 19: **Claudia and the Bad Joke**
No 20: **Kristy and the Walking Disaster**
No 21: **Mallory and the Trouble with Twins**
No 22: **Jessi Ramsey, Pet-sitter**
No 23: **Dawn on the Coast**
No 24: **Kristy and the Mother's Day Surprise**
No 25: **Mary Anne and the Search for Tigger**
No 26: **Claudia and the Sad Goodbye**
No 27: **Jessi and the Superbrat**
No 28: **Welcome Back, Stacey!**
No 29: **Mallory and the Mystery Diary**
No 30: **Mary Anne and the Great Romance**
No 31: **Dawn's Wicked Stepsister**
No 32: **Kristy and the Secret of Susan**
No 33: **Claudia and the Great Search**

No 34: **Mary Anne and Too Many Boys**
No 35: **Stacey and the Mystery of Stoneybrook**
No 36: **Jessi's Babysitter**
No 37: **Dawn and the Older Boy**
No 38: **Kristy's Mystery Admirer**
No 39: **Poor Mallory!**
No 40: **Claudia and the Middle School Mystery**
No 41: **Mary Anne vs. Logan**
No 42: **Jessi and the Dance School Phantom**
No 43: **Stacey's Emergency**
No 44: **Dawn and the Big Sleepover**
No 45: **Kristy and the Baby Parade**
No 46: **Mary Anne Misses Logan**
No 47: **Mallory on Strike**
No 48: **Jessi's Wish**
No 49: **Claudia and the Genius of Elm Street**
No 50: **Dawn's Big Date**

Look out for:

No 51: **Stacey's Ex-Best Friend**
No 52: **Mary Anne and Too Many Babies**
No 53: **Kristy for President**
No 54: **Mallory and the Dream Horse**
No 55: **Jessi's Gold Medal**
No 56: **Keep Out, Claudia!**
No 57: **Dawn Saves the Planet**
No 58: **Stacey's Choice**
No 59: **Mallory Hates Boys (and Gym)**
No 60: **Mary Anne's Makeover**

# Goosebumps

**by R.L. Stine**

*Reader beware, you're in for a scare!*

*These terrifying tales will send shivers up your spine . . .*

*Available now:*

### Welcome to Dead House
Amanda and Josh think their new neighbourhood is creepy and wierd . . . *dead* wierd!

### Say Cheese and Die!
Does Greg's new camera predict the future . . . or does it *cause* bad things to happen!

### Stay out of the Basement
Are the plants in the Brewers' basement harmless . . . or is it turning into another little shop of horrors?

### The Curse of the Mummy's Tomb
There's no such thing as the Curse of the Mummy's Tomb . . . is there?

### Monster Blood
Evan's buys some Monster Blood from a toy shop, and at first it's fun to play with. But this stuff is no toy . . . this stuff is *bad*!

### Let's Get Invisible
Can Max and his friends stay in control of their "magic" mirror . . . or will it start controlling them!

*Look out for:*

**Night of the Living Dummy**
When Kris's twin sister, Lindy, finds a dummy in a skip, Kris decides *she* wants one, too. But she's going to *regret* that decision . . .

**The Girl Who Cried Monster**
Lucy's loves telling "monster" tales to scare people. But now she really *has* seen a monster . . . and *nobody* believes her!

**Welcome to Camp Nightmare**
There are some pretty bizarre things happening at Camp Nightmoon. Billy thinks it's more like Camp *Nightmare*!

**The Ghost Next Door**
Hannah can't be sure, but she thinks she's discovered a *ghost* next door . . .

**The Haunted Mask**
**Piano Lessons Can Be Murder**

# THE BABYSITTERS CLUB MYSTERIES

*Our favourite Babysitters are detectives too? Don't miss the new series of Babysitters Club Mysteries:*

*Available now:*

## No 1: Stacey and the Missing Ring

When Stacey's accused of stealing a valuable ring from a new family she's been sitting for, she's devastated – Stacey is *not* a thief! One way or another the Babysitters have *got* to find that ring and save the reputation of the Club . . . before it's too late!

## No 2: Beware, Dawn!

Just *who* is the mysterious "Mr X" who's been sending threatening notes to Dawn and phoning her while she's babysitting, *alone*? Dawn is determined to get to the bottom of this mystery, but she's *pretty* scared . . . what if she's in real danger?

## No 3: Mallory and the Ghost Cat

Mallory thinks she's solved the mystery of the spooky cat cries coming from the Craine's attic. It's a little white cat. The Craine girls name him "Ghost Cat". But Mallory can *still* hear crying and this time it can't be Ghost Cat. Will Mallory find the *real* ghost of a cat this time?

## No 4: Kristy and the Missing Child

When little Jake Kuhn goes missing, Kristy can't stop thinking about it. After all, she *was* the last person to see Jake before he disappeared. Now he's been gone for two days, and things look serious. Kristy makes up her mind. She *must* find Jake Kuhn . . . wherever he is!

## No 5: Mary Anne and the Secret in the Attic

Mary Anne is curious about her mother, who died when she was just a baby. But Mary Anne's dad won't talk about it, so she decides to find out for herself. Whilst rooting around in her creepy old attic, though, Mary Anne comes across a secret she never knew – one she wishes she'd never discovered . . .

*Look out for:*

## No 6: The Mystery at Claudia's House
## No 7: Dawn and the Disappearing Dogs
## No 8: Jessi and the Jewel Thieves
## No 9: Kristy and the Haunted Mansion
## No 10: Stacey and the Mystery Money

# Robert Swindells

"Faithful, fearless, full of fun,
Winter, summer, rain or sun,
One for five, and five for one –
THE OUTFIT!"

*Meet The Outfit—Jillo, Titch, Mickey and Shaz. Share in
their adventures as they fearlessly investigate any mystery,
and injustice, that comes their way . . .*

*Move over, Famous Five, The Outfit are here!*

### The Secret of Weeping Wood

In the first story of the series, The Outfit are determined
to discover the truth about the eerie crying, coming
from scary Weeping Wood. Is the wood really haunted?
Are The Outfit brave enough to find out?

### We Didn't Mean To, Honest!

The marriage of creepy Kenneth Kilchaffinch to snooty
Prunella could mean that Froglet Pond, and all its
wildlife, will be destroyed. So it's up to The Outfit to
make sure the marriage is off . . . But how?

### Kidnap at Denton Farm

Farmer Denton's new wind turbine causes a protest
meeting in Lenton, and The Outfit find themselves in
the thick of it. But a *kidnap* is something they didn't
bargain for, and now they face their toughest
challenge yet . . .